Jason's Miracle
A Hanukkah Story

Beryl Lieff Benderly

Albert Whitman & Company
Morton Grove, Illinois

Library of Congress Cataloging-in-Publication Data

Benderly, Beryl Lieff.

Jason's miracle: a Hanukkah story / by Beryl Lieff Benderly.

p. cm

Summary: Twelve-year-old Jason has ambivalent feelings about Hanukkah until he
finds himself transported back to the time of the Maccabean revolt in Judea.

ISBN 0-8075-3781-0

[1. Hanukkah--Fiction. 2. Jews--History--586 B.C.-70 A.D.--Fiction.

3. Time travel--Fiction.]

I. Title.

PZ7.B431475 Jas 2000

[Fic]--dc21 99-086328

Published in 2000 by Albert Whitman & Company,

6340 Oakton Street, Morton Grove, Illinois 60053-2723.

Published simultaneously in Canada by General Publishing, Limited, Toronto.

Printed in the United States of America.

10 9 8 7 6 5 4 3 2 1

The typeface is rendered in Poliphilus MT.

The design is by Scott Piehl.

For Dan and Alicia, my miracles.

—B. L. B.

∗ 1 ∗

JASON WAS DISGUSTED. It was cold, and getting dark, and the darker it got, the more the Christmas lights came on. The whole darn street was twinkling by the time he got to his corner.

Plastic Santa Clauses and choir boys glowed on lawns. Six-foot candy canes gleamed on porches. Blue electric candles flickered in windows. Many-colored sparkles winked from pillars and doors. It made him sad. And it made him angry. He wished he didn't have to walk home from Hebrew school just as it was getting dark at this time of year. But every Wednesday he had to go, right after public school let out. By the time Hebrew school ended two hours later, lots of the houses he had to pass already had their lights on.

It really got to him. All the talk about shopping

and parties and new bikes and computers and rollerblades, all those weeks of hoping and planning, bragging and comparing. Now that it was cold and wet outside, everybody had to spend most lunch hours cooped up in the gym, shooting baskets, and that meant lots of time to talk about Christmas. In the fall and spring, when the weather was good, all the guys would be out throwing forward passes or kicking goals or hitting line drives. No one would have time to talk about presents. In the fall and spring, no one was making their list and checking it even once.

He turned the corner and trudged up the street to his house. *It's easy to tell which one's ours*, he thought. *Just us and the Fishers and the Burgers don't have any lights.* And the Fisher kids even had one set of grandparents who had a Christmas tree.

But Jason knew that his folks were hopeless. He had asked, and his sister Lisa had asked, but he knew his folks wouldn't budge an inch on Christmas.

"It isn't our holiday," Dad would say. "It celebrates something in a different religion. It's all about something we don't believe. For us to celebrate Christmas makes about as much sense as a Christian observing Yom Kippur."

"But lots of people say Christmas isn't even all that religious," Jason would argue. "Some of my friends say that for their families it's mostly about presents and decorations."

"Maybe for some people, but it's really still a cele/bration of someone else's religious event."

Once when Jason was feeling especially ticked off, he'd raised the subject with Lisa.

"Give it up, Jase," she'd said. "Dad's not going to budge. I tried years ago. He's really into this miracle business."

"You mean that thing about the oil? Do you think he really believes that?"

"Probably not. Anyway, Rabbi Heller told us at teen group that the story isn't even in the Book of Maccabees. It seems to be a legend that developed later."

"See?" Jason had said irritably. "That's what makes me so mad. Dad can't really believe it. So why does he have to make such a big deal about it?"

"Listen," Lisa answered in the condescending, fake grown/up tone that really got on Jason's nerves, "this isn't about whether something really happened. How many people do you know who really believe in

Santa Claus anymore? But does that stop anybody?"

Jason had thought about that a minute and shrugged. It had been years since any of his friends had really waited for the sound of reindeer on the roof, but they enjoyed keeping the secret going for the younger kids.

"Jason, listen to your big sister for once," Lisa had gone on. "I talked all this over with Mom a couple of times. She says for sure it's not about the oil. It's that the miracle is the whole thing. Or the whole thing is a miracle." She'd given Jason a more serious look than she usually did. "But here's the deal: there's no way Dad's going to give in on this. You might as well stop wasting your time trying to convince him."

So this year, at the beginning of yet another Christmas season, Jason knew better than to ask. It even made him a little ashamed that he still wanted to. He wasn't a little kid anymore; he was studying for his bar mitzvah. He knew in his mind that he shouldn't want Christmas, that he shouldn't envy the Christian kids.

But he knew in his heart that he *did* envy his friends who would find a mountain of presents under their sparkling Christmas trees. And his envy made him feel he was letting his parents down. So when people went around school singing. "'Tis the season to be jolly," he didn't feel jolly. When they sang "I have a little dreidel" in music class, he knew it really was sort of a consolation prize so that the Jewish kids wouldn't feel bad. It all made him feel confused and sad inside.

He pushed open the front door. Mom's voice came from the back of the house. "Jason? I'm in the kitchen, dear."

She was sitting at the breakfast bar, polishing the brass menorah. Her hands, the cloth, and the counter were smeared with black from the polish. There was a smoky smell in the air and a draft from an open window. It wasn't the warm sort of smokiness that Jason imagined must float up from mellow Yule logs. It was the greasy sort of smokiness that comes from scorched cooking oil.

Mom noticed his sniffing and laughed. "Isn't that silly?" she said. "I burned the oil for the first batch of latkes. The doorbell rang, and by the time I got back from answering it, the oil was black."

Jason nodded glumly while visions of scrumptious magazine illustrations danced in his head.

Golden-brown Christmas cookies. Candy-studded gingerbread. Even sugar plums and flaming Christmas puddings, whatever they were. Not just some silly little fried circle of potatoes with applesauce. He didn't even *like* applesauce.

"But don't worry," Mom went on. "I threw out the burned stuff and used some fresh oil. The latkes are fine, just waiting in the oven. And I used Grandma's special recipe for the applesauce."

She stood the menorah on the counter and gave it a squint and a final rub. "We'll light the candles as soon as Dad gets home," she went on, as she carried the menorah into the dining room and set it on the sideboard under the window. He followed her and watched as she took a box of Hanukkah candles from a drawer and put it next to the menorah.

"The menorah looks nice, doesn't it?" she said, smiling. The chandelier lights glinted off the curving brass arms, but the menorah's shine was nowhere near as bright as the lights out on the street.

"Happy Hanukkah, dear," his mother said. She kissed him and went back into the kitchen.

* II *

B Y THE TIME the fourteenth set of head‑
lights had streaked across Jason's bedroom
window, he thought he'd try lying on his
other side. It was awfully late, and he had discovered
again something he had known for a long time: you
can't get to sleep by trying to.

He felt dismal. He didn't know whether to be mad
at himself, or his father, or things in general. The fam‑
ily had gathered around the menorah and recited the
blessings and sung the songs. Mom had served the
latkes and applesauce. Dad had gotten sort of worked
up about the crispy little potato cakes.

"Really good this year, honey," he had said to
Mom as he finished off his plate.

She'd laughed and told him about the burnt oil.

"Well, that's only natural," he had said with a grin. "This holiday is about burning oil," he'd gone on, warming to his topic. "Burning oil that does the job."

"Oh, Dad," Lisa had groaned. "Why do you have to make every little thing so important?"

"Well, what could be more important than remembering miracles?" he had said. "That's why we eat latkes—because they're cooked in oil. Because they remind us of the miracle of the lights. Even the letters on the dreidel say it: 'A great miracle happened there.'"

So what! Jason had thought. That was ancient history. This was here. What difference did some old legend make to him?

"But Dad, we talked about that at teen club," Lisa had said with a laugh. "The rabbi told us the story of the light lasting for eight nights is probably only a legend."

Dad had laughed himself. "Maybe so. But there's more than one kind of light. There's the kind that you can see with your eyes, and then there's the kind that you feel inside of you."

Jason smiled, though, when his parents gave him a nice pair of binoculars. Dad at least had picked up on his hints about wanting one for hikes with his scout troop. Then the family had played some rounds of dreidel and munched on some chocolate gelt.

Jason sat up in bed. *Well, maybe I can have a Christmas tree when I grow up and have my own house*, he thought. *Dad's always saying that when I have my own house I can do things however I want to.* But Jason didn't like himself when he thought that way.

He punched his pillow. Maybe another glass of water would help.

He climbed out of bed and shuffled toward the bathroom by the orange glow of the little hall night light. Mom and Dad and Lisa were asleep and the rest of the house was dark. Except...

As Jason passed the top of the stairs, he thought he saw a light below. He was almost sure it hadn't been there the last time he'd gone for water. No, something was different...

He stopped, bent over the bannister, and peered down the stairs. There definitely was a dim flicker.

Maybe something's on fire, Jason thought, moving quickly down the stairs to check. It couldn't be a candle, he knew. They had lit only one tonight, along with the shamash light, and both the flames had gone out hours ago. The little supermarket candles didn't even last an hour.

At the bottom of the stairs he saw that the light was brighter, and that it came from the direction of the dining room. The fire—if that's what it was—couldn't be very big yet; he hadn't even noticed any smoke. Maybe he could still put it out. He dashed into the dining room but stopped short in surprise.

There, in front of the sideboard where Mom kept the good silver, crouched a complete stranger. The cabinet doors were open, and the intruder was rummaging around inside. Light poured over the person from the lighted menorah on the sideboard. All nine candles blazed.

"Hey, what's going on here!" Jason barked, stepping into the pool of light. The intruder whirled around, startled.

It was a boy about Jason's own age, with thick, dark hair hanging to his shoulders. He looked jumpy, ready to bolt, but not sure which way to go. "Who are you?" he snapped.

"Who are *you*?" Jason snapped back.

The boy looked very strange. A cloth band tied across his forehead held his heavy hair off his face.

Above bare legs he wore a sort of short skirt made of rough, light-colored fabric; a shirt of the same material hung loosely around his body. He wore sandals with straps that wrapped almost to his knees. His deeply tanned face showed surprise, puzzlement, and eagerness but no fear.

"Why, I'm Aaron. I thought you were expecting me. I'm Aaron ben Moshe. I was sure you knew I was coming."

"*Expecting* you? I never heard of you!"

"But isn't this the Cohen house?"

"Yeah, but what's it to you? Talk, or I'll call the police."

"The police? You mean the government authorities? Please, not that!" Aaron said urgently. "That would waste my whole trip. I had a really hard time getting here. I've never been here before, and everything is strange. I even had trouble getting inside, until I found an open window. Then I found this lamp"— he motioned to the menorah—"and I lit it so that I could start looking for supplies. But I couldn't find anything."

"Why are you looking for stuff in my house?" Jason demanded.

"Well, like I said, I thought you knew I was coming. They told me back at headquarters that people named Cohen—members of the priestly tribe—would want to help our cause. But now you say you're going to call the police. If I wanted to be arrested by the authorities, I'd have stayed at home in Judea!"

"Judea?" Jason said in confusion. The only time he'd heard of Judea was in Hebrew school. It was an old name for a part of Israel. "Don't you mean Israel? Do you mean you came from Israel?"

"No, not Israel," Aaron answered brusquely. "Judea. Occupied Judea. Occupied by the Syrians."

"You're crazy!" Jason said. His mind reached back to what Mrs. Lerner had told the class. Now he wished he had listened better. "You can't be coming from there now! That was a thousand years ago! Two thousand maybe!"

"I don't know what you're talking about," Aaron said coldly. "It sure seems like now to us. One thing I do know: if we don't get help, our revolt will fail."

"Your revolt? *What* revolt?"

"Don't you know anything?" Aaron looked annoyed. "The revolt of the people hiding in the hills. The revolt of the rebels fighting for our freedom—

for our right to live and practice our own religion in dignity."

"But..."

"Listen," Aaron said, "if you don't think that's important, I can go somewhere else. If you don't think it's worth fighting for, I'll stop wasting my time. We think it's important enough to risk our lives. The Syrian pigs are trying to destroy our people and our way of life. They want us to worship their filthy Greek idols. They make us keep their holidays and don't let us celebrate our own. They kill people who circum-cise their sons or worship God in our way. They've got the people so scared that lots have already given up our religion."

Jason, confused, searched Aaron's flushed and excited face. The strange boy seemed perfectly sincere and his story sounded familiar, somehow. Jason tried to think of where he had heard it before. Whatever Aaron was up to, Jason felt sure that it must be impor-tant and that he meant no harm. "I don't understand," Jason said at last. "Why did you come here?"

"They sent me through the lines to get supplies and help. There aren't that many of us in Judea who stand with the Maccabees."

Jason's head was reeling. "You're with the *Maccabees*?" This Aaron was totally weird! And even weirder, if he was from far away, from a long time ago—how could Jason understand what he was saying? How could Aaron understand him? Yet somehow they could speak to each other.

But Aaron's excitement was catching, Jason realized. He suddenly noticed that his own heart was racing so fast that he could hardly get his words out. "You want my help?"

"You're a Jew, aren't you?" Aaron asked simply.

"Sure I'm a Jew. But what can I do?"

"Plenty. We need supplies: food, bandages. We need people to join us. If we don't get help soon, our army will fall and we'll all die and our religion will die with us."

The desperate urgency of Aaron's voice began to convince Jason to help this strange, anxious boy get what he needed so he wouldn't let down whoever he thought was depending on him. If those people weren't the Maccabees, then who could they be? And what was really going on? Jason knew it might be risky to find out. But he knew he had to take that chance. He just had to know what Aaron was mixed up in.

"Okay," Jason said. "I'll do what I can."

"That's great," Aaron said, a smile cutting the tension on his face. "Thanks, uh…Thanks a lot."

"My name's Jason. You were right—I'm Jason Cohen."

Aaron put out his hand in a gesture of gratitude, but Jason didn't stop to shake it. He was already on his way to the the hall closet, where he grabbed his backpack off the floor. For good measure he also grabbed the bag lying next to it, an old one that Lisa now considered too geeky to take to high school. In a moment Jason was in the kitchen, stuffing the packs with bread, cheese, bananas, peanut butter, whatever he could find. Aaron watched in puzzlement as Jason grabbed a bag of bagels from the freezer.

"What's that?" Aaron asked, reaching tentatively toward the plastic bag.

"It's bagels—a kind of bread."

"But the pieces seem to be inside some kind of a sack," Aaron said. "And yet I can still see them."

"What do you expect? It's plastic," Jason answered, sticking the package into the backpack and moving on toward the bathroom.

"Plastic?" Aaron asked as he followed.

Jason was too busy scanning the medicine chest to answer. He scooped up bandage strips, adhesive tape, gauze pads, a roll of cotton, antibiotic cream, tissues, a washcloth. Aaron watched curiously.

"There," Jason said at last, "food and first aid supplies."

"Could we also take along some of the amazing oil you use here?" Aaron said. "Getting oil for our lamps can be a real problem."

"Oil?" It was Jason's turn to be puzzled.

"Look at how brightly that lamp shines." Aaron pointed to the bathroom light.

"But that's not—" Jason started to say. Then he looked again at Aaron's stubborn expression and decided this was no time for a science lesson. "Sorry, we can't take any of that," he said. "It's...it's too hard to carry."

But talking about carrying light reminded Jason of something else. Returning to the kitchen, he took out the flashlight Mom kept there for emergencies and stuffed it into a pack. Then he picked up the new binoculars from where he'd left them on the kitchen table and added them to his gear.

"I'd better get dressed," Jason said.

"No time," said Aaron, who had already opened the door.

Jason shrugged, shouldering his pack. Then, handing the other bag to Aaron, he followed him out into the night.

✶ III ✶

AT FIRST JASON THOUGHT he'd show the way since this was his own neighborhood. But Aaron, a strong, confident, tireless scout, quickly took the lead. They moved down Jason's street under the light of an enormous full moon. All the houses were dark. None of the Christmas lights twinkled now.

They made their silent way first through familiar streets, past Jason's school and the shopping center and the synagogue. Aaron stopped for a moment to stare at the big aluminum menorah standing on the lawn with two of its electric bulbs lit.

"That's our synagogue's menorah," Jason explained.

"But it has eight branches," Aaron objected. "The one in the Temple in Jerusalem has six."

"Well, it's a special menorah," Jason stammered. "It's really for Hanukkah—for the miracle of the lights."

Aaron looked skeptical. "Never heard of that miracle," he declared. "Are you some special kind of Jews?"

"No, no," Jason said. "We're just ... " But Aaron's gaze was now fixed on the two granite tablets that decorated the building's front wall. The engraved Hebrew letters of the commandments, embossed in gold paint, shimmered in the moonlight.

"Isn't that awfully risky," Aaron asked, "having Hebrew writing right out there where anybody can see it?"

"Why risky?" Jason said. "Who cares? Who'd object?"

"You mean it's OK for you just to be Jewish? They don't forbid it?"

"Why should anyone forbid it? I don't understand ... "

"There's a lot you don't understand," Aaron said grimly. He shot Jason a sharp, level look, as if taking his measure. Then he turned and continued swiftly down the street.

Soon they were passing through increasingly unfamiliar streets, and then through parts of town Jason had never seen before. At last, when they got to the edge of town, to where Jason knew the ball field should be, it didn't seem to be there. Instead, there was a darkened countryside completely unknown to him. Overhead more stars than Jason had ever seen sparkled against a sky as black as black velvet.

It seemed to Jason he had never walked so far, never covered so much ground. He followed closely behind Aaron, who walked swiftly in determined silence. But Jason's pack never felt heavy, and he never felt tired or cold as he moved through the darkness.

Then their path narrowed and steepened, and Aaron put a finger to his lips in a signal that Jason should be very quiet. The land was dry and rocky and their route, a barely visible indentation in the brown dirt under the full moon, threaded through a forest of scrubby trees.

"We're in enemy territory now," he heard Aaron whisper, his first words since the synagogue lawn. Jason hunched over close to the ground as he followed Aaron silently up the trail.

At last Aaron stopped and crouched behind a big rock that overlooked a narrow clearing. Signaling Jason to squat down next to him, he whispered, "Almost there now."

Jason heard someone moving nearby. Peeking over the rock, he saw a shadowy figure stalking in the moonlight. "That's our sentry," Aaron mumbled. "Follow me." He stood up and stepped into the clearing.

The guard instantly turned to face them, and Aaron threw out his arms to protect Jason. The man was big and muscular with a heavy beard. His clothes were similar to Aaron's, though he had some kind of leather protector strapped to his chest and lower legs. A wide sword hung from his thick belt, and he held a shield.

"Who goes there?" he called out.

"Friends!" Aaron shouted back.

"Hands up! Stay where you are!" cried the sentry. He drew his sword. A second armed, shielded man appeared from behind a tree.

But Aaron took a step forward and the men gave him a nod of recognition. "Who's that?" the first guard asked, cocking his head toward Jason.

"A friend," Aaron said, "with supplies."

"Well, take him to Judah," the man said. "And Aaron," the man smiled, "welcome back."

Aaron again plunged into the woods, taking a path so narrow that Jason could hardly see it, much less follow it without tripping. They soon came to another, larger clearing. Tents stood here and there, and about a dozen men sat around a small campfire talking intently. All wore some version of Aaron's outfit—a shortish garment and sandals. Some had leggings, some chest protectors, one or two wore a helmet. Nearly every belt carried a sword or dagger or both. As Aaron and Jason approached, several men, hands to their weapons, sprang to their feet and advanced threateningly toward the boys.

"Eliezer," Aaron called hastily to the man closest to them, "It's me, Aaron—Aaron ben Moshe. I've brought help."

Eliezer's stern face melted into a grin and he embraced Aaron, a bit roughly but affectionately. *Eliezer*, Jason thought, *that name's familiar* ... Then he remembered: Eliezer was one of the sons of the priest Mattathias, the old man who had begun the Maccabean revolt by defying a Syrian order to worship a Greek idol. Eliezer was among the small band Mattathias had led to the hills to prepare their fight for freedom.

Eliezer was strong and bearded, about Jason's dad's age or a little younger. His dark eyes were at once lively and watchful. "Glad you got back safely," Eliezer said warmly, giving Aaron a friendly pat on the shoulder. "We need you. And everyone else who will join us." Then he turned a curious gaze to Jason. "Who is this you've brought?"

Before Aaron could answer, a deep, resonant voice called from the campfire. "Eliezer, bring them over here."

Hearty greetings and more welcoming shoulder pats awaited Aaron when he reached the group, now all on their feet. "Welcome back," said the man who had called out. "We were beginning to wonder. Your mission took a bit longer than we had expected."

"I know, General," Aaron said.

Could this general be the famous Judah Maccabee? Jason thought as Aaron continued talking.

"The territory was pretty hostile," Aaron said, "and I had to travel a good deal farther than we had originally planned before I found what I was looking for. But it was worth the effort in the end. I brought back a good man and some supplies."

"Let's see who you've brought," the deep voice went on.

Aaron gave Jason a little push in the general's direction. As Jason stepped forward he looked up into the strongest, most commanding face he had ever seen. It was lined and deeply tanned, and the dark eyes shone in the firelight. But Jason could see that they burned not from the reflected campfire but from their own inner intensity. He couldn't make out the jawline under the heavy beard, but the mouth was full and firm, the gaze direct. Judah's individual features were very much like Eliezer's, but they combined to make a face that was more handsome, more balanced, in some indefinable way more mature and impressive. Jason could see why people called this man "the Hammer."

Jason took another step toward Judah Maccabee, squared his shoulders, and tried to make his voice sound as if it had already changed. "Mr. Maccabee," he began. "I mean, General Maccabee, sir, I'm Jason—"

"Jason!" Judah snarled. His hand went instantly

to his sword. "Aaron, I thought you were smarter than that! What do you mean bringing a Greek, an enemy, to our camp! You showed him the way!"

Already, the other men had surrounded Jason, drawing their swords and daggers. "No, no, General!" Jason gasped. "Jason is just my cover name! My Hebrew name is Joseph! I'm Joseph ben David HaKohen."

"That's better," Judah said, dropping his hand from the hilt of his sword. The other men relaxed a bit, but Jason thought that Judah was probably never completely at rest. "You understand, Joseph, that we can't take any chances here. We have few friends and many enemies. But we're glad to have you among us.

"Tell me, Joseph," he went on, "who is your father, David HaKohen? What is his complete name? I know many members of the priestly tribe. Perhaps I know him."

"No, sir, General, I don't think so," Jason stammered. "He is David ben ..." He thought for a moment. Grandpa Cohen's name was Sam. "David ben Shmuel. He doesn't live ... um ... around here. I don't think you ever met him."

"Well, perhaps someday I will," Judah said.

"Perhaps father and son will both join our fight."

"Oh, I don't think he'll be coming here," Jason said. "He's kind of busy and kind of far away…"

"You mean he doesn't support our cause?" Judah's voice was harsh.

"Oh, no, sir, he's a big fan of yours. I'd say he's one of your biggest fans. He's on your side one hundred percent. I mean, he just can't leave my mom and my sister."

"Understandable enough!" Judah said. "Family is very important. In fact, our work here is really a family affair. All my brothers are here with me, you know. In fact, I want you to meet Johannan, Simon, and Jonathan." Three of the men in the group—Jason could see the family resemblance—nodded in turn. "And I want you to remember," the general went on, "that our father, Mattathias—of blessed memory—started this struggle of ours. It's already gone on for several years."

"Oh, yessir, General, I know that. We learned about him in Hebrew—I mean, I've heard about that."

Judah gave Jason a pointed, inquisitive look before going on. "My father would be glad to know that

Jason's Miracle: A Hanukkah Story

others of the priestly lineage are coming forward to join our cause. He was outraged that some priests have let themselves be won over by our enemies. He could never understand how descendants of Aaron could bring themselves to carry out the rituals of our oppressors. He insisted on doing what he thought was right. Some people thought he was unreasonable and unbending in his ideas. There were those who thought he should be more flexible, more adaptable, adjust his views a little more to changing circumstances. Sometimes it was not easy to be his son."

"Yessir," Jason said quietly. "I see what you mean."

"But in the end," Judah continued, "he was right to stand up for his beliefs and right to urge us to do the same. And because of that, in the end, I deeply believe that we will prevail. Yes, indeed, Joseph, I believe that we will one day enter the holy Temple in Jerusalem. And when we do, you will go ahead with the *Kohenim*, the other priests."

"With the other priests?" Jason blurted out. He had never thought of Cohen as being more than a name that had an ancient story attached to it, but here, in Aaron and Judah's country, the name made him a

27

priest, and that meant something important. It all seemed very strange.

And it seemed even stranger that this little band of men, who were barely holding their own and needed all the help they could get, would ever achieve any legendary victory.

Judah seemed to have read his thoughts. "I know that for the moment it looks as though our dream can-not be realized," the general said. "But we have faith that things will improve for us. We have faith that if we all do our best, we *will* win our way back to the Holy City, we *will* restore the Temple to God's ser-vice. Or we will all perish trying."

Jason was amazed that Judah could have such confidence in himself, his companions, and the right-ness of his cause. But suddenly he realized how little he really understood of what was happening to him or around him. Maybe, Jason thought with alarm, he shouldn't even be so sure that that Maccabees would in fact win. Certainly Aaron had said they could lose. Everything that had happened since he met Aaron had been so strange that there seemed no telling what the future would bring...

"So, Joseph," Judah was saying, "what have you

brought us? I see that you and Aaron are both carrying heavy burdens."

With a start, Jason pulled himself back from his thoughts. The men gathered around as he and Aaron unloaded the food and first aid supplies onto the ground. Jason watched Judah Maccabee tentatively inspect a jar of peanut butter. The general looked it over top and bottom, hefted it in his hand to judge its weight, then tried to pry the lid off with his fingers.

"No, sir, you turn it."

Judah's eyebrows arched as Jason demonstrated. The men murmured. Jason held the open jar to the puzzled commander. "It's called peanut butter, sir. You eat it on bread."

Judah warily dipped a finger in the shiny paste, then nodded as he licked.

The other officers watched intently. Then they scanned the collection of supplies spread before them on the ground. Simon bent down and gingerly grasped a banana. Frowning, he felt it with both hands. "And this?" he said. "It has the shape of a clever projectile, with points at the ends. I think it would spin if I threw it. But I don't think it can be a weapon because it feels soft."

Jason stifled a grin. "You're right, sir, it's not a weapon," he said. "It's a fruit. You take off the yellow." He snapped the end and pulled down a strip of the skin, exposing the white inside. The men all muttered appreciatively as Jason broke off pieces and passed them out for everyone to taste. "The only thing dangerous about a banana is maybe its peel."

Judah studied Jason for a long moment. Then he studied the open jar, the empty peel in the boy's hand, and finally, the array of objects still on the ground.

At last he said, "We are glad you have joined us, Joseph. We can see that you have come from a distant land. And we are grateful that you have brought us these useful things from your own country. But now it is late. Aaron will show you where you can sleep." He signaled to the men. "We must all get some rest. We have much to do in the morning."

Jason bedded down on some blankets near the campfire next to Aaron. This time, he had no trouble falling asleep.

✳ IV ✳

T HE SUN WAS JUST peeking over the
horizon when Jason opened his eyes,
awakened not by the alarm clock this
morning but by Aaron shaking him. Jason blinked
in the almost-dark of daybreak and sat up slowly, his
muscles stiff from sleeping on the hard ground.

The camp was already abuzz with activity. Jason
yawned and stretched in his bedroll, obviously one of
the last to awaken. All around him, men were straight-
ening their tents or strapping on their swords and body
armor or assembling their gear into bundles. As the
light increased, Jason could see that the camp extended
a good distance beyond the campfire circle he had seen
last night.

Dozens of tents stood in neat, military rows. Some were rather splendid little structures—stolen from the Syrians, Aaron explained—while others were much more modest assemblages of cloth and wood, and some had obviously been put together out of branches, mended blankets, and other things scrounged around camp. A little way off, a group of soldiers practiced with swords and spears under command of their officers. Just like the group around the fire last night, Judah's men wore their own clothes rather than real uniforms. Some had apparently either captured or scavenged pieces of clothing, sandals, or other equip⁄ment from their well⁄supplied enemy.

"Good morning," Aaron said with a broad smile. He stood over Jason with a pair of thick sandals in one hand and a tunic in the other. "Got to get you out of those clothes," Aaron said. "They'll attract the wrong kind of attention."

Jason looked down and, with a laugh, discovered he still had on the T⁄shirt and sweatpants he had worn to bed. Moments later, though, with the sandals strapped to his feet and a belt about his waist, he could have passed for a brother of Aaron's who happened to have short hair.

Then Aaron led him to the command tent, where Judah sat with several officers studying maps. His orders to Aaron were brief and to the point. Then he looked speculatively at Jason.

"Are you sure it's wise to take Joseph along on this mission?" the commander asked. "Perhaps he needs a bit more time to become familiar with the terrain."

"I'm positive he'll be an asset, sir," Aaron said. "He's smart and resourceful. I saw that last night."

So the general nodded his approval and sent the boys on their way.

And so, with the sun no higher than it usually stood when Jason set out for school, Jason was moving quickly alongside Aaron, down a dry, scrubby hillside toward Bet Tzur, a walled valley town he could see in the distance. Their assignment, Aaron explained, was to spy out information about enemy strength in and around the town so that the general could find out just how outmanned the Maccabean army really was.

I'm not much of a spy, Jason thought. But then, he realized, it really isn't much of an army, either. The history he had heard at Hebrew school was coming back to him. He remembered reading that most of

Judah's men were volunteers with no military experi⁄ence. Instead, they were ordinary farmers, shepherds, and merchants who had become soldiers by drilling in the hills with the Maccabees and fighting against the Syrians. Judah himself wasn't a trained officer, simply a man with a talent for strategy and a gift for inspiring others.

Altogether, they reminded Jason of what he had learned in school about the American Revolution and the ragtag army Washington had led. Judah's men had slipped away from their homes, one by one or in small groups, to join the rebels in the hills. And like Washington's forces, they had stuck by their com⁄mander through some pretty hard times.

"What we find out today could really make a dif⁄ference," Aaron said as he shifted the heavy load of firewood on his shoulders. Jason also carried a big pile of sticks that they had picked up. His shoulders and back were starting to ache from the weight. But he couldn't put the wood down because it was part of his disguise. He and Aaron would try to enter the enemy⁄occupied town posing as farm boys with firewood to sell in the market. A cloak covered the short tunic that had replaced his clothes from home. Under it he also carried his backpack with bread, cheese, and fruit for lunch.

Aaron hitched his own cloak forward to cover most of his face. They were passing through the town gate now, hoping to melt into the stream of pedestrians, horsemen, and donkey carts on their way to market.

Jason's heart began to beat faster. A large Syrian soldier stood in their path, under the heavy stone arch of the main gate in the city wall. He looked enormous in his metal helmet and breastplate. He clanged his tall spear on the cobblestones. "You boys there! Where are you going?"

"To market, sir," Aaron said meekly, "to sell our firewood."

The soldier looked them up and down. "Long live the Emperor Antiochus!" he cried.

"Long live the Emperor Antiochus!" Aaron answered smoothly, not missing a beat as he pronounced the hated tyrant's name.

The soldier waved them on. Aaron led the way through narrow, dusty streets lined with stone houses, mostly built closely together. Men and women in cloaks and flowing garments, boys dressed rather like themselves, and young girls with long, wavy hair all made their way in every direction on foot, atop horses and donkeys, or in wagons and carts. Sweating youths pushed laden hand carts. Children darted among the passing figures. Babies clung to big sisters or rode serenely tied in mothers' shawls. A teenage girl moved lithely under a large earthen jar balanced on her scarf-covered head.

It wasn't easy to carry the ungainly bundle of sticks through such a thick crowd without bumping into anyone. From time to time, Jason's sticks brushed against an arm or leg or back and he murmured an apology. Once he nearly toppled a frail old lady and reached out frantically to steady her.

Aaron seemed to be having better luck. But then he got too close to the girl with the jar, and a stick protruding from his pile bumped into the arm she was using to hold her burden in place. The jar swayed, and Jason was sure it would crash to the cobbled street. Luckily, though, she quickly raised her other hand and stabilized it.

"Are you all right, Miss?" Aaron asked.

"Yes, I'm fine," she said. She was just about Lisa's age.

"I'm very sorry," Aaron went on. "It was clumsy of me. The streets are so crowded on market days."

"Yes, they are," she said, her gaze cool and non-committal.

"Well, I'd better get on to the marketplace," Aaron said. "Again, I'm very sorry."

"No harm done," she said, and went on her way.

"We'd better watch it," Jason said. "That was a close call."

"Yes, it was," Aaron answered, a half-smile on his lips.

A few more twists and turns through the maze of the town brought them abruptly into an open square even more densely packed with people than the streets had been. Here the crowds moved among rows of little stalls piled with vegetables, grains, chickens in cages, pots, fruits, eggs, cloth, tools, sandals, dishes, spices, and a riot of other goods.

To Jason it was an overwhelming scene, but Aaron moved confidently through the crowd, not stopping until he reached an alley at the market's far end, barely wide enough for him to squeeze into. With Jason right behind him, he ducked in and let his load of wood drop to the ground, signaling to

Jason to do the same. "Whoever finds this won't have to collect firewood today," Aaron said with a laugh.

Then he quickly led Jason back through the marketplace and out into a street on the side opposite where they had entered.

"Now to get to work," Aaron whispered.

Jason followed him through a tangle of small streets, up alleys, across little plazas, in and out of buildings. In many of the squares Jason saw great statues of Greek gods that the Syrians had erected and forced the Jews to worship. In front of some of the houses stood small stone tables that Aaron whispered were pagan altars. It shocked Jason to see townspeople—their fellow Jews, Aaron said—kneeling without resistance and making offerings to idols large and small. "It seems like more and more people think copying Greek religion is safer or easier than sticking to ours," Aaron said bitterly.

As the two boys crossed a small square, they saw a group of young Syrian soldiers overtake an old man. The aged man moved along slowly, creakily, his bent shoulders making him look even smaller than he really was.

"Well, Grandfather," one of the soldiers said, prodding the old man with his spear, "are you ready to worship the great god Zeus?" He poked the man again and all his friends laughed.

Jason stiffened. "They can't do that!" he said loudly. He noticed that no one was coming to the old man's aid, that in fact most of the people in the plaza were quickly making themselves scarce. He took a step toward the aged Jew. Aaron grabbed Jason's arms hard just above the elbow. "Easy," he whispered. "Don't attract attention."

Jason tried to wriggle free. "But look what they're doing to him! Shouldn't we—"

"No!" Aaron cut him off with a sharp, fierce whisper, keeping his grip on Jason's arms. "We should stand here as if nothing is happening."

The old man kept on his way, ignoring the soldiers.

"Oh, you're deaf, are you, Graybeard?" the first soldier shouted. "Come, pray that Zeus will restore your hearing." All the soldiers laughed even harder, and two of them grabbed the old man's arms, nearly lifting him off his feet. They dragged him toward an idol standing in the square and pushed him to the ground in front of it. One held a spear at his back.

Now, for the first time, the old man spoke. "Hear, O Israel," came his voice, high-pitched yet surprisingly firm as he pronounced the age-old prayer, "the Lord our God, the Lord is One."

"So you do have a voice, Graybeard," snarled the soldier with the spear. He raised it and struck the old man. Jason could see blood in the old man's white hair as he fell forward onto his face. The soldiers laughed, harder than ever.

Aaron had pulled Jason back into a doorway and was holding him there by force, his hands like iron around Jason's arms.

"The pigs!" Jason spat the words. "Why do people let them get away with that! Why didn't we do something!"

"Like what?" Aaron asked. "Attack their spears with our bodies? Then who would spy for Judah?"

Aaron's words hit Jason like a slap across the face. He forced himself to take two or three long breaths. "I guess you're right," Jason finally answered, burning with shame and frustration.

"Anyway, that sort of thing has been going on for years."

After the soldiers had moved on and people had come hesitantly forward to carry off the old man, the two boys slipped unnoticed up the street. All that remained of the incident was a stain of blood on the statue's base.

Jason still seethed with anger, but Aaron, apparently calm, was peering sharply here and there, his eyes noticing, counting. There were more and more Syrian soldiers in this part of town, Aaron explained, because they had commandeered a number of buildings for their garrison. Everywhere that Aaron saw soldiers he tried to count them.

"I wish I could count faster," he said glumly. He pointed to a detachment of troops moving down a street. "See them all? But how can I ever add them up fast enough? Look, there are 8 in a row. I count 32 rows. Two 8s are 16; another 8 is 24; 8 more is 32. See, it's impossible!"

Jason thought a moment. "Two hundred fifty-six," he said.

Aaron stared at him. "What did you say?"

"I said there are 256 soldiers. Plus the sergeant, of course."

"You know this for sure?"

Now it was Jason's turn to be puzzled. "Sure," he said, "I did it in my head, but I can write it down if you want." He picked up a stick and began to scribble in the dirt. "Look: 8 times 2 is 16. Put down 6 and carry 1. 8 times 3 is 24, plus 1 is 25. That comes out to 256."

"But that's wizardry," Aaron gasped. "It's a miracle."

"It's no miracle. It's multiplication."

"I have no idea what you mean, Joseph. I have no idea what is signified by those marks you made. I only know that we had better remember those numbers so that Judah can know exactly how many Syrian soldiers there are in this town."

"We won't have to memorize them," Jason said. "I'll write them down."

"Don't make jokes," Aaron snapped. "This is serious! How can you possibly write? We can't carry an ink pot on a mission like this. And we can't afford a parchment or even a papyrus."

Jason slipped his backpack from his shoulders. He usually used it to carry his school stuff, and, sure enough, he found a pencil at the bottom. Then in one of the pockets he found a crumpled piece of paper, a sheet from his Hebrew school notebook, covered with tic-tac-toe games. He quickly erased them.

"Okay," Jason said, "What's the name of this place? Street of the Bath? All right—256 soldiers."

Aaron said nothing. His mouth hung open in amazement. He stared at the pencil and paper as if they would reveal the secret of the universe.

"You can write," he asked, his voice hushed with awe, "without ink? You carry parchment around with you? You make those few little marks to recall the numbers to you?"

It was Jason's turn to stare back. "Of course. It's nothing special."

"Oh, no, Joseph. It's a miracle."

Before long, Jason's sheet of notebook paper carried a complete rundown of Syrian forces in and around the town.

"We'd better get back, don't you think?" Jason asked as he tucked the precious page into his backpack.

"Not yet," Aaron answered. There's something else we've got to do." And he led Aaron through another tangle of streets, finally stopping before a small shop. Row upon row of sandals in all sizes lined the cobblestones before the establishment's narrow front. Leather belts and bags of every description hung from the walls. A strong, musky scent of leather filled the air.

Aaron paced thoughtfully before the array of footwear, now and then squatting to examine a particular sandal. "What do you think of this one?" he asked in a loud voice, handing a shiny brown model up to Jason.

"Aaron, have you gone nuts?" Jason said. "Why are you wasting time looking at shoes?"

Aaron shook his head ever so slightly and hissed a "Shh!" between his teeth. "Or do you think this one is better?" He went on in the same firm conversational tone. "Don't you think this color is nicer?"

"Oh...they're both nice," Jason answered vaguely, keeping a close eye on Aaron. "I guess it depends on which one—"

"Can I help you?" a friendly female voice cut in. Jason looked up to see a girl—in fact, the very same girl whose jug Aaron had almost overturned—coming toward them from the back of the shop. "We have a number of other kinds besides those," she went on smoothly, as if she had never laid eyes on either of them before. "And of course my father can custom-make any style you wish. We have some lovely leathers in stock right now."

"Custom-made?" Aaron said, standing up and taking the sandals from Jason. "That's an interesting idea."

Jason looked from one earnest face to the other. Why on earth this inane conversation about shoes when there was important work to do?

"I'm sure he'd be glad to make a pair exactly the way you want them," the girl continued. "Why don't you step into the workroom at the back of the shop and discuss it with him?"

"That's a good idea. Come on, Jason," Aaron said, emphasizing the Greek name, "you can help me decide what to order."

The girl stepped aside to welcome them into the shop. Aaron entered and cocked his head to a mystified Jason to follow. The two of them went ahead of Jason, toward a door at the end of a long narrow shop, talking intently about colors and textures of different leathers.

The girl rapped on the door. "Father," she called in a loud voice, "there's a customer who wants to see you about a special order."

After a moment came the reply, "Show him in, Melissa!" She pushed the door open and the boys stepped into a workroom full of the rich smell of new leather. A man and two teenage boys sat at cobblers' benches cutting or stitching pieces of leather.

The three workers facing them did not move a muscle or say a word, but each held a sharp metal tool in a strong hand and watched the new arrivals closely. Jason could read nothing in either their features or their body language. He took a step backward, thinking he'd leave the strange group in the gloomy room. But the girl, Melissa, had come up behind him, shut the door and bolted it with a thick piece of wood. And in the folds of her garment, he saw in a sidewise glance, she fingered a sheathed dagger.

* V *

ARON!" SHOUTED the shoemaker. Jason suddenly realized how big and muscular he looked.

The man and his two young helpers leapt up from behind their benches. Jason braced himself for an attack, but the three dashed toward Aaron only. To Jason's surprise, the man embraced Aaron in a bear hug. The two older boys pumped Aaron's hands and pummeled his back. And Melissa began to laugh and dance around with excitement.

"Aaron!" The man roared again, "How wonderful to see you! You got here safely!"

"Menachem!" Aaron gasped, laughing and catching his breath at the same time. "It's great to be here! The plan worked great!" He managed to extricate himself long enough to motion toward Jason.

"This is my friend Joseph HaKohen, alias Jason," he shouted over the din of happy voices. "Poor guy, he's been standing here wondering why I was sud⁄denly so interested in shoes."

"A real pleasure," said the shoemaker, releasing Aaron and extending a friendly hand toward Jason. "I'm Menachem, alias Menelaus in Greek." The man who moments earlier had been silent, wary, and forbidding now had Jason's hand in a strong, two⁄handed grip. "Always glad to meet anyone working for the cause. These are my apprentices, Saul and Caleb. And I think you've already met my daughter Miriam—alias Melissa."

The girl beamed at Jason with the same slightly mocking but affectionate big⁄sisterly smile that he recognized so well from home. "I think Joseph really thought that Aaron suddenly wanted to buy shoes!" she laughed. "I could see him standing there won⁄dering whether Aaron had lost his mind!"

"You owe that boy an apology," Menachem boomed.

Aaron turned to Jason and grinned. "I sure do! The plan was for us to come here to rest up and get the news from Menachem to take back to Judah. But

I didn't dare tell you—I didn't want to risk being overheard. And I didn't know for sure that the meeting was on until I ran into Miriam—*really* ran into her—this morning."

"That's our prearranged signal," she explained. "In the mornings I have to go down to the fountain near the marketplace to get water, so I look around to see if anyone has come here from Judah. The messengers kind of accidentally on purpose bump into me to let us know to expect them here at the shop later on. Everybody who comes here about the cause uses buying shoes as a cover," the girl went on. "We work the conversation around so that they have to visit the workshop, either for a custom order or to have a repair made."

"And sometimes," Menachem said jovially, "someone comes here who isn't working for the cause, and we actually sell a pair of shoes!"

"It's perfect," Miriam went on, "because it's impossible for any outsider watching to tell who is a real customer and who isn't."

"Now, boys, we'd better get down to business if you're going to get out of here tonight," Menachem announced. He walked toward a round table at the back of the room. Covered to the floor by a dark cloth, it held an assortment of tools, a sloppy pile of copper coins, and an oil lamp. Clearing off the tools, he motioned them to sit.

"The windows, Miriam," he murmured. His daughter quickly pulled heavy curtains across the two openings that looked out onto the alley behind the shop, so that only dim light filtered through. "Saul, Caleb," he said, "we need Miriam here, and there's nobody outside minding the store. Could you two take over for a while?"

In an instant the two apprentices were out the door. "It's not that I don't trust them," Menachem explained to Jason in a low voice. "They and their families are solidly with the cause. It's to protect them—and us. The less they hear, the less they can inadvertently let slip. I wish I could do the same for Miriam," he said, lovingly patting his daughter's hand, "but she's the best spy we have here in town. Somehow," he added with a wink, "she gets soldiers to say things they'd never tell me."

"Just luck, Abba," Miriam said with a demure smile. "Ima finds out lots of interesting stuff, too."

"It's true," Menachem said. "My wife, Sarah, is a

marvel at picking up bits of information, especially in the market. She goes to buy vegetables and comes back with details about the enemy's strategy."

"I've watched her do it," Miriam said. "She just stands there examining eggplants or olives, and men don't pay her any attention. They just talk as if she weren't there. They assume that she's an ordinary housewife buying groceries and couldn't possibly understand or care or remember what they're talking about. But she understands and remembers everything."

"She'll be sorry to have missed you boys," Menachem said. "But she's gone to Hebron with the baby, on a special mission carrying some messages back and forth. Of course, she makes a perfect courier. She has relatives all over the country—her sister Deborah lives in Hebron—and the enemy never imagines that a mild-looking, motherly lady traveling with her little son could be up to anything.

"I only wish that I was as good an agent as the women in my family," he went on. "I was supposed to get Judah information about the army's strength here in town, but I just haven't been able to. I have a cousin who sells wine to the garrison and gets to go in everywhere, but he's been sick the past week or so and hasn't been able to get around."

"Don't worry," Aaron beamed. "Joseph has a complete count of all their units."

Menachem's eyes widened. "What?"

Jason reached into his pack for the piece of notebook paper. As Jason peered at the rough pencil marks in the darkened room, Menachem struck a spark from a pair of tiny flints and lit the oil lamp. Its flickering flame gave Jason just enough light to make out the words and numbers.

"It's a marvel," Menachem said at last, a moment or two after Jason had finished reading off the list. "Aaron, you've been in town only this one day. How did you gather all this so quickly?"

"Because of Joseph," Aaron said proudly. "Joseph and his wonderful way of adding faster than the eye can see. It takes me forever to add up large groups, but with him I would only say, there are 19 groups of 12 men, and in a flash he would tell me the number. I don't know how he did it."

"And these figures are exact, Joseph?" Menachem asked.

"Absolutely, sir. I got an A in math last term."

Menachem gave Jason a curious look that made Jason hold his breath. At last he said, "I do not know what you mean, Joseph, or how you do this thing. But I do understand what it means to Judah, to the army, to all of us. Judah is such a brilliant strategist that if we have a way of letting him know our enemy's exact strength, it will almost assure our victory."

"Gee, I don't know...," Jason said, embarrassed.

"No false modesty, Joseph," Menachem commanded. "You bring an extremely powerful possibility to a cause that needs help and encouragement. But you know," he went on enthusiastically, "I am becoming more and more hopeful every day. There are more and more signs that righteous people can overcome tyrants."

Menachem reached under the tablecloth and pulled out what looked like a small, very thin Torah scroll. Jason saw that it had the same shape as the sacred scrolls in the synagogue ark back home, though it was plainer: no silver crown, no velvet covering. Almost automatically, as he would have when the Torah was taken out in the synagogue, Jason scraped back in his chair and began to stand, but none of his companions budged.

"Is something wrong?" Menachem asked. "Do you need anything?"

"No," Jason stuttered in confusion. "Shouldn't we...uh...?"

"Don't worry," Menachem said amiably, plunking the scroll on the table and rolling it open. Columns of black Hebrew letters, just like those Jason could see when the scroll was lifted before the congregation during services, marched before his eyes. But unlike the words he'd studied with the cantor for his bar mitzvah, these were not neat and perfect. Here and there the writer had scratched out a mistake. Most of the writing looked hurried and sloppy; occasionally a black splotch marked the spot where the scribe must have used too much ink.

"Have you heard of this wonderful new book?" Miriam asked excitedly. "It tells how Daniel and the other righteous people were able to survive in the days of the Babylonian exile when they faced problems as terrible as those we face now. They were brave and devoted and stayed faithful to our religion even though they had been conquered by a mighty enemy."

"Daniel?" Jason muttered. "You mean Daniel with the lions and the dreams?"

"You've read it, Joseph? You know it?" Menachem asked. "Isn't it great? We were absolutely thrilled when we heard the story. The book has just been discovered. It all happened hundreds of years ago, but nobody had heard of it until the last few months."

"And we're so lucky that a friend was able to lend us this copy for a while," Miriam added. "There aren't many around—you know how long it takes for a scribe to write out the whole story. And it's really risky to be caught copying a Hebrew book."

"You mean someone has to write each word out by hand? That must take forever!" Jason said.

"Well, how else would you make a book?" asked Menachem, puzzled. "There isn't any other way."

"No, I guess not," Jason said quietly, almost to himself. Obviously they couldn't use a copying machine or a printing press or a computer printer! Books took on a whole new meaning if each one had to be laboriously hand-lettered by a man dipping a primitive pen into an inkwell, just like a scribe had done for the Torah scrolls in the Aron HaKodesh back home. He could see how this kind of book would be very precious indeed.

"Do you know a better way of making books,

Joseph?" Menachem asked. "We would love to be able to have more."

"No, not really," Jason mumbled, thinking of all the cheap paperback books he had thrown away.

"Well, we're lucky and grateful to have this one," Menachem enthused. "It's really terrific. Look!" he said, thrusting a finger at one of the columns of print. "This is one of the best parts. See how Daniel's friends, who refuse to bow down to the tyrant's idol, are saved from the fiery furnace! And Daniel himself is saved from the lions! And Daniel has visions that foretell the triumph of the righteous over their persecutors! Why, he might have been talking about us! Look, Aaron! Look, Joseph! How can you read this and doubt that our cause will—"

A sharp cry from the outer part of the shop interrupted Menachem. "Master! Master!" came a squeaky, quavering voice. Then a crash and a shout, and the door flew open.

* VI *

SAUL AND CALEB hurtled into the room, as if propelled by a great force. And, indeed, two large, burly Syrian soldiers shoved in right behind them. Jason stared in horror. Saul lay sprawled on the floor, where the soldiers' fierce push had landed him. Caleb was still on his feet, but his eyes were wide with fear. No one had bolted the door when the apprentices left the room, Jason suddenly remembered. And now, here they were, with this incriminating book on the table!

"Master!" Caleb wailed, "We tried to tell them you were busy."

Menachem, already on his feet, coolly walked over to where Saul lay, squatted down, and lifted the boy's face. His cheek was bloody and swollen. "Melissa!" he called. "Get some water to clean his wound."

"Yes, Father," Miriam said, as calmly as if the visitors were old friends.

"Calm yourself—I'm sure you did your best," Menachem said to Caleb. Then he stood up and turned to the soldiers. "Tell me, Sergeant, in what way can we help you? Do you wish to try on some shoes?"

"Shoes, my eye," the larger of the soldiers grumbled. "I want to know what you all are doing here in this back room in the middle of the day."

"Why, Sergeant, I was just taking a little break from my work. My nephew here came to visit," he said, indicating Aaron, who nodded, "along with his friend." He indicated Jason, who did the same. "And we were amusing ourselves with a harmless little game of chance."

Jason glanced down at the table. To his relief, the scroll was gone, whisked back to its hiding place under the table. In its place at the center of the table sat the mound of coins.

"See," Menachem went on, holding out his open palm. In it, to Jason's amazement, lay a small, four-sided top carved of wood. "The boys enjoy spinning this top to see how it will fall. I'm afraid that sometimes we even bet on which side will be uppermost."

"I don't get it," the sergeant barked. "That is such a stupid game, but all you Jews seem to play it. Half the time we see a group of you, you're playing that silly game."

"You're right," Menachem said blandly. "I agree that it's not that interesting a game, but all the young people seem to enjoy and spend time playing it. You see, there's a mark on each side, and how much you win or lose depends on which one comes up. Now, some of the boys even try to perfect their spinning technique to beat their friends, but personally I don't think—"

"Enough," the sergeant said. "We didn't come here to discuss games. We came here because there seem to be a lot of people coming to this shop, a lot of people from out of town, and not very many buy shoes. We want to know what's going on."

"So do I," Menachem sighed. "It is very puzzling to me. Perhaps I have chosen the wrong styles. Or perhaps it's my prices. I know my quality is good...you think my prices are too high?"

"I don't think so, Uncle," Aaron volunteered earnestly. "I think your prices are very reasonable."

"Oh, for Zeus's sake, I didn't come here to talk about shoes, either," the sergeant growled. "I came to make sure you weren't up to any funny stuff."

"Oh, Sergeant," Menachem said with a weary smile, "I wish that I were having some fun. But you know, these days the life of a poor shoemaker is not easy. What with taxes, and business being poor, and all the disruptions caused by this silly rebellion, it's getting harder and harder for an honest man to make a living that will support his family. The other day my wife was telling me about the prices in the market. You wouldn't believe how much the farmers want for fruits and vegetables these days, she says. Of course you can't blame the country people for being afraid to come into town very often. With these crazy rebels running around the countryside, an honest person can't feel secure. Why, just the other day—"

The sergeant snorted. Menachem seemed likely to go on chattering all afternoon. The sergeant clanged his spear handle on the ground. Menachem stopped talking. "Tell me, Shoemaker," the Syrian said in a quiet voice that nonetheless carried a tone of threat, "if business is so bad, and you are having such a hard time, why do you burn oil in your lamp during the day when you could easily let in the natural light?"

"The lamp?" Menachem said tensely. "The lamp?" He paused the merest instant before going on in his former, jovial manner, "Oh, that lamp? I was doing some very fine stitching, and I couldn't see to do it without some extra light. My eyes aren't as good as they used to be. You know how it is when people get older—well, perhaps you don't, yet. And of course, seeing clearly is very important to do my best work, so I often have to light the lamp during the daytime. Of course, my apprentices don't have that problem. Like you, they're young and—"

"Oh, for great Zeus's sake, that's enough!" the sergeant shouted. Menachem's mouth snapped closed. The Syrian took a few paces around the room, throwing suspicious glances here and there. Finally he said gruffly, "You can go about your business." He and his partner turned to go.

"Caleb, show the gentlemen out," Menachem said mildly.

Caleb scampered through the door and bowed from the waist. "This way, please."

The minute the two soldiers had crossed the threshold, Aaron sprang forward to close the door behind them.

"Not so quickly," Menachem whispered through his teeth as he stood in the doorway smiling and bowing slightly to the departing Syrians, whom Caleb was courteously escorting to the street. After they left, the boy stood for a moment bowing after them, and then began to walk slowly toward the back of the long narrow shop. But his pace picked up the closer to the door he came, and he ran the last couple of steps and jumped joyfully into the workshop.

"Now!" Menachem said, and Aaron slipped the bolt. "Well done, everyone," he said, laughing. "That could have been close." Then he turned toward Saul, still lying on the floor, but with Miriam kneeling at his side bathing his cut cheek with a damp cloth.

"I'm okay, Master," the boy said cheerfully. "It doesn't hurt too much. It's only a scrape and a bruise."

"It doesn't seem to be serious, Abba," Miriam agreed, "even though it must feel sore."

"He's hurt enough for a little time off, anyway," Menachem said kindly. "Caleb, why don't you take Saul and help him get some rest?"

As the two boys left the room, Jason, who had been watching everything in silent amazement, finally spoke up. "I'm not sure I get what's going on here," he said. "You get together to study forbidden Jewish books, like this Book of Daniel?"

"Yes, everyone wants to read it," Miriam said.

"And if the Syrians come," Jason went on, "you pretend to be playing a gambling game with a top?"

"Isn't it clever?" Miriam asked happily. "The tops are really cheap to make. And the best part is that the soldiers all gamble a lot, so they always believe that everyone else does, too. I think it's just amazing how they think we want to be like them. They're so sure…"

A knock at the door silenced her.

"Master," came Caleb's voice after a moment. "It's getting dark now. Do you want me to close the shop?"

"Closing time already?" Aaron spoke up. "I really would like to read this book, but I think we're going to have to get back to camp this evening. Judah's expecting us."

Menachem frowned, eased the door open a crack, and peered out. Closing it, he said, "He's right, Aaron. It's really starting to get dark. Are you sure you want to try to get back tonight? You don't want to go wandering around in the hills at night, and you know they're on the lookout for our people. That means you can't carry a torch or a lantern. They're sure to see it."

This puzzled Jason. "What's the problem?" he asked Aaron. "We got around fine last night."

Aaron shot him a warning look. "That was different," he said. "Last night we weren't so close to the soldiers."

"Abba, I'm worried," Miriam chimed in. "Remember how Ima sent word that there are a lot of patrols out on the roads? Maybe it's not a good idea for them to travel tonight."

"That's certainly true," Menachem said thoughtfully. "Nighttime might be just too dangerous."

"Well, we can't travel tomorrow in the daylight," Aaron said. "We came into town pretending to be firewood sellers from the country heading into market. All the real country people have already left for home; they certainly wouldn't stay in town overnight without some very good reason. There's no choice. We've got to go now."

Jason remembered the flashlight in his backpack. "Aaron," he said confidently, "Don't worry. I think we'll find our way just fine."

Aaron looked at him. "You think so?"

Jason winked. "I'm sure of it."

Menachem and Miriam started to object, but the

boys insisted. "We'd better say good-bye here, then," Menachem said. "Can't risk being seen in the shop." He reached under the table for a small sheet of papyrus that he rolled up and handed to Aaron. "Take this note to the general, if you don't mind. It has some information he needs." Aaron nodded and tucked it safely under his belt. Then a round of hugs and fervent good wishes sent Jason and Aaron on their way.

"God be with you," Menachem whispered to them as he opened the door a crack. Caleb stood waiting in the gathering gloom, a lighted lamp in his hand.

"And with you," whispered Aaron and Jason as they slipped through the door to the darkened shop. The apprentice led them down toward the street end of the narrow stall. The sandals hanging from hooks by their long straps and the belts and harnesses along the walls cast weird shadows in the flickering light.

When they reached the street, Caleb said in a clear, firm voice, "I look forward to seeing you again when the sandals you ordered are ready."

"So do I," Aaron answered.

Aaron and Jason stepped onto the street.

"Thanks to you both," Caleb nodded, starting to

pull together the heavy night shutters that would close off the shop. As the panels began to swing shut, the boys could still see Caleb's face illuminated by the lantern light. He mouthed *Good luck!* Then the sliver of light vanished between the closed shutters and they heard him slide the bolt on the inside.

Aaron stood frowning in the dark, looking at the rows of blank, shuttered fronts of merchants' and artisans' stalls that lined both sides of the street. No moon or stars shone in the overcast sky. No streetlamps lit the walkway, and from inside of the nearby houses came only the occasional weak flicker of an oil lamp. Jason remembered Menachem saying oil was expensive. It didn't seem like many people could afford to burn it. Working, reading, even playing a game of dreidel after dark must be a sheer luxury, Jason thought.

"I don't know how we're going to find our way back to camp," Aaron whispered glumly. "We certainly can't use a torch without being seen, and there aren't any stars or moon for us to see by tonight."

"I told you not to worry," Jason said, and slipped the flashlight from his pack. Aaron gasped as a yellow beam fell on the rutted ground before them.

"It's a...it's a miracle," he said, his voice hushed.

"No, it's a flashlight." Jason snapped the light off. "Come on, Aaron, let's get going."

Quickly and quietly they made their way toward the city gate they had entered that morning. Jason briefly clicked on the light a couple of times to help them find their way. Almost no one else moved about in the darkened streets. But several times they glimpsed pairs of Syrian foot soldiers patrolling the town. The soldiers' loud voices and the sound of their swords slapping their legs or their spears clanging on the street gave the boys plenty of warning to scamper up an alley or hide in a doorway so as not to be seen.

When Jason and Aaron finally came within sight of the town gate they found, to their relief, that it stood wide open. In the light of several clustered torches, four very large soldiers, equipped with what seemed to Jason to be very wide swords, very thick chest armor, and very long spears, stood guard at the main portal, an opening in the thick stone city wall wide enough for horses and wagons to pass through. But the guards were paying no attention to a narrow, enclosed passage that ran right alongside.

"We're going to have to get through the smaller passage when they're not looking," Aaron whispered.

"I've done it before, so I know it's possible. They're not guarding it that strictly because they don't think anyone would try to leave the city on foot at night."

It's easy to see why, Jason thought, as he looked out at the dark, rocky wasteland that stretched beyond the gate.

"Come on," Aaron whispered, signaling Jason to follow him into the passage while the guards were huddled together in a group, their backs turned, apparently occupied by a gambling game. As quietly as they could, the boys raced the short distance to the pedestrian passageway. But once inside, they had to slow down. The stone-lined passage stretched before them about fifty paces, Aaron explained. That meant fifty paces of complete, inky blackness. Jason reached for the flashlight.

"Wait!" said Aaron. "Don't—"

But Jason knew he'd never make it through the passageway if he didn't have some idea of what lay ahead. He flicked on the light for the tiniest instant.

In that same second, a cry went up from one of the guards. "Look," he shouted to his comrades, "What's that light over there?"

In the totally darkened town, the brief flash of

Jason's beam had reflected off the entrance's stones and caught a guard's attention. The guard reached for a torch, and in seconds he and another man were in pursuit.

Aaron and Jason fled through the dark before them, Jason shining the flashlight to show the way. Jason had never before been so scared. This was a really bad fix, he knew, and one that could even be fatal—not only for him and Aaron, but for Judah's chances of capturing Bet Tzur and for lots of their friends. If he and Aaron were captured, neither the notebook paper nor Menachem's note would reach Judah. And the Syrians would get solid proof of what they already seemed to suspect: that Menachem, Sarah, and the rest of their household were working for the rebels. Everything hung on the boys' ability to outrun the two soldiers who were rapidly gaining on them.

Suddenly the passage took a sharp turn to the right. Jason, veering abruptly, slipped on the damp stones and fell onto his stomach. The flashlight flew from his hand and went out. He could hear pencils, pennies, and other junk from his open pack hitting the stone floor.

"Joseph, what's wrong?" Aaron called as he dashed ahead. "The light—"

"I fell!" Jason yelled back. "Don't stop!"

Groping desperately in the dark for the flashlight, Jason suddenly touched something round, soft, and squishy. A banana, left over from the loot he had shown to Judah, now lay squashed on the stone floor. He tossed it over his shoulder with one hand, feeling frantically for the light with the other. A second later he gripped the hard tube and was on his feet, racing after Aaron He shook the light violently as he ran, and, amazingly, it came back on.

But he could hear the Syrians right on top of him. The light from their torch flickered off the walls. "Keep going, Aaron!" he yelled. "You get away if you can—"

A loud crash and a furious shout from behind drowned out his words. Then a second huge crash and a scream echoed off the passage walls. Racing for his life, Jason saw that the light from the Syrian's torch was no longer gaining on him, and the pounding of the soldiers' feet had stopped. The passage rang instead with angry shouting.

Jason dashed out of the passage and kept running

for a distance on the open plain.

"Joseph!" Aaron's hoarse whisper came from behind a large rock where he crouched, panting. "What on earth happened in there?"

"I don't know," Jason whispered back, breathing hard. He squatted down beside Aaron, out of sight of the passage entrance. "They stopped coming right after I got up. It's almost as if—they tripped."

Then he yelled joyously, "That's it! They did trip!" Laughing out loud, he said, "One of them must have stepped on the banana! I must have thrown it in their way! And then the second one must have tripped over *him!*"

Aaron was shaking his head. "I don't understand," he said. "What's a banana?"

Jason stuck his hand into his backpack. "This!" he yelled as he pulled another one out, bruised but whole. "The peels are incredibly slippery," he gasped when he could finally stop laughing. "It's almost impossible to step on one and not fall."

Aaron looked at him quizzically. "That was brilliant, Joseph," he said at last.

"No, that was a piece of dumb luck," Jason answered. "And even luckier, the rest of the guards don't seem to have noticed anything." Peeking around the rock, he could make out the two remaining Syrians still lounging in the firelight next to the main portal. The passage's thick stone walls must have had muffled the noise of their comrades' disaster. "We'd better get out of here before they do."

But Aaron didn't move right away. "It's amazing," he said. "You're full of miracles."

"Not really," Jason laughed, peeling the banana.

"Yes, really," Aaron said. Jason just smiled and popped the sweet fruit into his mouth.

✳ VII ✳

JUDAH MACCABEE, deep in conversation
with several of his officers, looked up eagerly
as Aaron and Jason approached the campfire
circle. "Back so soon, boys? How was it in Bet Tzur?"

"Interesting, General," Aaron answered with a
grin.

That's one way of putting it, Jason thought, remembering their narrow escape.

"And we really made good time on the way back,"
Aaron went on. Jason estimated that it was well past
midnight. He couldn't accurately tell the time from
the sky the way his new friends could, but he did have
some notion of how long he and Aaron had been traveling since they left Menachem's.

"We have great information," Aaron added

enthusiastically. And, to the amazement of all, Jason read off his list of numbers and locations, giving Judah a complete rundown of the enemy's strength in Bet Tzur. During the recitation, Aaron beamed with pride, almost as if the astonishing piece of paper were his own invention.

"Remarkable," Judah said at last, shaking his head reverently. "Just remarkable. I have no doubt now that Bet Tzur will be ours, and when it is, the road to Jerusalem will lie open."

The officers nodded in agreement. They all wore dazed expressions, as if they had watched a magic trick they could not possibly explain.

"That is an unbelievable day's work," said Judah.

"But there's more!" Aaron blurted out joyfully. "A letter from Menachem!" And he thrust the precious papyrus into Judah's hand.

The general carefully unrolled it. He squinted at the writing, trying to make out Menachem's message by the wavering firelight. Jason stepped over beside him and snapped on the flashlight. A gasp went up as the yellow beam fell on the slip in Judah's hands. The men all stared at Jason and at the bright orange cylinder in his hand.

"It's just a kind of lantern we use back where I come from," Jason explained. "Please, General, read the letter. I don't want to keep it on too long. It wastes the battery." They stared at him, mystified. "I mean, it uses up all the fuel."

"That's how we got back here so quickly," Aaron added. "Joseph's wonderful lantern showed us the fastest way."

Judah let his eyes rest a long moment on Jason's face and then turned them toward the letter. He frowned as he read it. "This is very serious," he said when he finished reading and Jason had snapped off the light. "Menachem warns us of a great army under the Syrian commander Gorgias, encamped not far from here. He says that a very reliable source—I sus⁄pect he means his wife, Sarah—guesses their strength at about six thousand men, including a thousand horsemen. And they are very confident that they will defeat us. Menachem writes that their general has even invited slave dealers to follow his army because he's so sure that he'll take lots of us prisoner. A force so much bigger than ours is a real threat to our plans."

The officers all nodded gravely.

"They really have us greatly outmanned,"

Jonathan said. "There's no way we can match those numbers."

"We don't have any cavalry to speak of," Simon added. "And their equipment is so much better than ours."

"All true," Judah said. "Their force is superior to ours in almost every way."

But the news didn't seem to dishearten Judah, Jason noticed. The general was quiet for a moment. Then he said, "We'll just have to come up with a superior strategy to defeat them."

The men murmured assent. But from their expressions, Jason suspected that some were doubtful.

Still, Judah seemed to relax a bit. "Anyway, I don't think anything will happen just yet," he said. "Right now," he went on, smiling at Jason and Aaron, "you two must be very tired. Go get some rest."

Aaron gratefully stretched out on his blanket, closed his eyes, and fell asleep. But Jason felt too keyed up to think of sleeping, feeling a jumble of fear, excitement, elation, and anxiety. The day's adventures still raced through his mind. He decided to walk around a bit. He strolled until he reached the encampment's edge, where the rocky hillside fell away in a steep cliff broken only by jutting ledges. It gave a panoramic view of the plain below.

The moon had come out now, and the landscape stretched toward the horizon in the silvery light. As his eyes gradually adjusted to the dark, Jason could make out the features of the plain in more and more detail. A patchwork of farmers' fields, groves, and pastures was dotted here and there with clusters of buildings. No lights illuminated these villages since the farming people were probably in bed. After a while his eyes were attracted to a larger group of much smaller structures that gave off a faint glow.

Jason took a deep, satisfied breath as he gazed out over this toy landscape, which looked from the height of the mountain about the right size to sit beside an electric train set. And he thought of all the people who would rise to do their work as soon as the sun came up and they didn't have to burn their precious fuel to provide light.

Suddenly Jason sat upright. His eyes went back to the patch of land giving off the glimmer of light. Clearly those people, unlike their neighbors, were keeping a number of fires going through the night—

He reached into his pack and pulled out the

binoculars. Peering through them, he quickly saw that the area was not composed of clustered houses but of rows of tents. The faint glow came from many distant campfires.

Instantly he was on his feet, and moments later at the door to Judah's tent. "General," he called. "I think I've spotted the Syrian camp!"

Almost as quickly, Judah was up, wiping the remains of sleep from his eyes. Jason led him quickly to his vantage point. Judah looked out sharply toward the dimly glowing rectangle that lay miles away on the plain.

"Joseph, you must have amazingly keen eyes. You're right. That is certainly the Syrians' camp."

"It's no big deal, General," Jason said. "I have a good pair of—I mean, I have a very good pair of eyes."

"So I see, Joseph. Tell me, can your very good eyes detect whether the Syrians are up to anything?"

"Uh, General, I'm going to try to get a closer look from that ledge there." Jason didn't know how he could possibly explain the binoculars to Judah. The flashlight appeared to be merely a strange kind of lantern to the men of the Maccabean army, but they had nothing at all like binoculars. "I'll let you know," he called as he climbed down to a stone surface that jutted out several yards. Judah remained, scanning the distant view from his place above.

In his new position, Jason again raised the binoculars to his eyes. Gliding them toward the Syrian encampment, he suddenly found himself looking not at the motionless rows he had seen before, but at a busy anthill. Tiny figures bearing tiny lights moved about rapidly, most of them concentrating at one end of the camp.

"General," he called, "they're moving around."

As Jason watched, the masses of tiny figures formed into lines, then into blocks that began to flow across the landscape in the direction of Judah's camp. "General, a whole lot of them are coming this way. They look like they're in formation."

"Are all of them coming, or do you see some staying behind?"

As Jason watched, the main body of the group moved away from the rows of tents. A number of the tiny forms, however, stayed behind. "Yes, sir," he said. "It looks like some of them are staying."

Judah stood for a moment as still as a statue, his eyes intent, his masterful face motionless.

"You are absolutely certain, Joseph?" he called gravely. "This is a very, very dangerous situation. Could there be any mistake?"

Jason watched the mass of tiny figures move steadily closer and then returned his gaze to the few still in the distant camp. "No, sir. There's no mistake. They're coming. At least most of them are."

Judah came closer, but said nothing for some time. He, too was peering sharply out over the plain, his eyes squinting. "I would never have been able to recognize what was happening if your excellent eyes hadn't spotted it first," he said. "Now that you point it out, I see that you are absolutely right." Now the general was all action and determination. "Come, Joseph. We have no time to lose."

In minutes the Maccabee camp was awake and Judah was giving orders to his massed forces. "The Syrians are moving against us from their camp near Emmaus," he announced. "I suspect they think they can take us by surprise. But instead of trying to fight a much larger force here, we are going to make a little surprise of our own. At least we're going to surprise the forces that they have left in their camp. The Syrians look like they are going to come up the front of this hill. We, meanwhile, are going to go down the back before they get here.

"I know I can count on each one of you to do your duty for the cause," he went on in a stirring voice. The men looked at one another and nodded resolutely. "I am going to lead our forces out of our camp. I want it to look deserted, as if we fled from them in fear. But we need to know what happens here, so my two expert secret agents, Joseph and Aaron, will stay behind. They will hide on that ledge above our camp and watch what the enemy does when he arrives."

Jason felt a stab of disappointment: he was going to miss the main action. As the soldiers formed up to march out, he went to Judah, who was busy giving specific orders to various officers. Finally Judah noticed Jason.

"General, sir," Jason began, "I was wondering whether I couldn't be useful during the march. You, know, with my good eyes I could—"

"No, Joseph, I need your good eyes here. This maneuver calls for experienced fighting men. But we won't know for sure if it worked unless someone watches here."

"But, General, if Aaron and I are separated from

the army, how will we ever meet up with you again?"

"I wouldn't worry about that, Joseph," Judah said. "If my strategy works, you'll see us back here in the morning. And if it doesn't—well, you'll be better off as far from our army as you can be."

And so, before the Syrians were halfway across the plain, Judah's plan was underway. As the Maccabean army set off down the hill, Jason and Aaron clam-bered up to the ledge overlooking the deserted camp. Peering down on the rows of empty tents and smol-dering campfires, Jason still wished he could have gone along with the troops to see the battle. But, Aaron pointed out, they did a vital job just by waiting in their secret lookout.

"We ought to watch in different directions so we don't miss anything," Jason suggested, moving a short distance from Aaron and settling into a spot hidden from view by some spiny bushes. Then he focused his binoculars on the action unfolding on the plain. He could see the Syrian forces grow steadily nearer and the glow of their torches steadily brighter. Then he shifted all the way around and could just make out Judah's men moving in the opposite direction. Before long, though, Jason didn't need magnification. He could hear, and then see, the enemy approach. He stowed his binoculars in his pack and crept over to the rock that hid Aaron. "They'll be here in a minute," he whispered.

"I know," Aaron whispered back.

Despite Jason's pounding heart, and his suspicion that Aaron's was beating every bit as fast and hard, he lay perfectly still, hidden from the Syrian view by the rocky cliff edge. Aaron, lying beside him, could have been carved from stone.

Together they watched the emperor's soldiers sweep into the Maccabees' ragtag camp. *You'd certainly never mistake these guys for Judah's forces,* Jason thought. For one thing, they were all large, muscular, well-groomed, and well-fed. No farm boys or grandfathers, or men with limps or bad eyes who had joined up because they believed in a cause. And the Syrians' helmets, breastplates, shields, and weapons were sparkling, undented, and free of scratches, patches, and repairs. Everybody's uniform and equipment matched everybody else's. The officers didn't ride on tired farm horses; each sat on a sleek, vigorous steed outfitted with the very best gear.

The man on the largest, most spirited stallion

pulled to the front of the advancing column, accompanied by three or four mounted officers.

"That's their commander, Gorgias," Aaron told Jason in a whisper so quiet that Jason had to lipread the words.

"Nobody here, sir," one of the officers said to his leader.

"So," Gorgias announced with satisfaction, "the mighty rebel general, the one they call 'the Hammer,' has fled. No doubt they saw us coming and headed for the hills to save their miserable lives."

"Some 'Hammer,'" another of the officers said with a scornful laugh. "It won't be hitting us anymore!"

The others joined him in laughter.

"It certainly won't, especially after we track them down in the hills and destroy them," Gorgias agreed. "We outnumber them so badly that they won't stand a chance!"

Pressing his face to the ground to keep as still as possible, Jason suddenly took a breath full of dust. He coughed loudly as Aaron watched in horror. Gorgias stopped talking, and the officers with him looked around sharply. As Jason struggled to hold in the cough he could feel coming, Aaron frantically pressed both hands over Jason's mouth.

The next cough came as a muffled snort.

Aaron kept his grip as Jason's cheeks puffed out again.

The Syrians moved about on their horses, scanning the trees and the cliff face.

Aaron held on tight.

"Probably just a horse whinnying, sir," one of the officers said at last.

"It's not very likely the rebels would have left anyone behind," Gorgias agreed. "Not when they were running for their lives."

The others murmured agreement.

"Well, come on," Gorgias ordered. "Let's not waste any more time talking. I want to get this business over with as soon as I can."

"Should we destroy their camp, sir?" one of the officers asked.

"No, that can wait until after we find them," Gorgias said. "Better to do it later, after we've caught any stragglers who try to return here."

Orders were quickly given, and the Syrian forces, with Gorgias at their head, moved off at double time in exactly the opposite direction from where Judah was heading. The horses were galloping, and the foot soldiers had to jog to keep up.

As the last Syrians passed out of earshot. Aaron released his hold on Jason, and Jason gave a mighty cough. Both boys whooped joyously and pummeled each other, laughing uncontrollably.

"They've gone off on a complete wild goose chase!" Aaron finally managed to gasp. "They'll never find Judah, and he can do what he wants to their camp." And he added, "I hope I didn't hurt you."

"No harm done. You had no choice."

It was hours before the boys knew what Judah had in fact decided to do. About dawn, looking through the binoculars, Jason saw the mass of Judah's army reach the Syrian camp. A scene of confused and frantic action followed. Jason couldn't make out who was who from such a distance, but a bevy of tiny figures, rather like a swarm of bees, soon fled the enemy camp.

"Gosh, I hope those guys running away are Syrians and not ours!" he cried.

But then, not long after that, Jason spotted another group approaching. "Uh-oh! Gorgias's army is coming back to their camp!" The Syrian commander had obviously given up the hunt in the hills and circled around toward home.

"But don't you think Judah will do something to stop them?" Aaron asked.

"I sure hope so," Jason answered, "but I don't know what it can be. There are so many more of them than of us!"

But as the Syrians came near, their camp suddenly burst into huge flames.

"Look at that!" Aaron yelled as a dancing orange mass and great columns of smoke rose into the clear sky. "I knew Judah would do something!"

And before their eyes Gorgias's army, until then so orderly and disciplined, fractured into a chaos of startled men and terrified horses racing off in every direction.

Jason and Aaron could hardly believe the way the great enemy force seemed to melt away without a fight. They were even more amazed at the huge supply of equipment that Judah's army brought back to camp later in the day. Many of the men sported new shields, helmets, and swords. Captured Syrian horses strained to carry loads of weapons, armor, and gear. Judah had even found bags of silver and gold left by the fleeing slave traders. These, he announced, would buy plenty of food and medical supplies.

Joy was unrestrained in camp that night. And as word of Judah's stunning triumph spread among the people of the plain, more and more men hurried to join the cause of freedom.

Around the general's campfire, toast after toast was drunk and cheer after cheer raised to Judah's breath-taking strategy.

"Judah," said a laughing Eliezer, raising a cup of wine to salute his brother, "I couldn't believe they fell for it!"

"All those men, and all those horses, and they walked right into your trap!" Jonathan cried.

"They may have the numbers and the money, but we've got a genius for a general!" Eliezer held his cup high. "Gentlemen! Let's drink to the boldest, most brilliant general that ever led an army to victory!"

Judah seemed embarrassed by so much praise. "I am only one person fighting for the cause," he insisted. "Everyone's contribution is important. And some of our people, don't forget, have already given their lives for freedom. Many of our supporters have suffered to maintain our religion and our cause in the face of the enemy's persecution. We need everyone, all of you, if we are to win. Why, if the trumpeters hadn't played so ferociously when we got to the Syrian camp, the soldiers left to guard it wouldn't have woken up scared out of their wits and frantically run away. I would never even have thought of setting this trap if I hadn't known that the Syrians had moved most of their forces out of their own camp, so that there was only a small force left guarding it. We have to say that we wouldn't have won without our trumpeters, and we wouldn't have won without Joseph, our most excellent spy."

It was Jason's turn to be embarrassed as the men gave him a cheer and Aaron proudly thumped him on the back. "General, I really didn't do anything," Jason stammered.

"Joseph, you're much too modest," Judah beamed. "Your information was crucial to our oper-ation today. And it will be to our next operation, too. All that stands between us and Jerusalem is Bet Tzur. Thanks to you, we know the enemy's strength there. Thanks to you, we'll crush them there, too."

✳ VIII ✳

T O JASON IT SEEMED an eternity of waiting. But before dark fell he and Aaron, watching the battle of Bet Tzur from a hill overlooking the town, heard a great cheer. They knew that Judah's prediction had come true.

They raced to the gates of the liberated town, this time finding them guarded by smiling members of the Maccabean army. People leaned singing from windows, they danced in the streets, they tossed flowers on the victorious army from the rooftops. People hugged the soldiers as they passed. A lovely girl ran up and threw her arms around Aaron and then kissed Jason on the cheek. He usually didn't care much about girls, but this time the kiss felt wonderful.

The air was filled with singing and laughter and repeated crashes as the hated idols were toppled to the ground. Menachem and Miriam, Caleb and Saul, along with a woman who Jason guessed was Sarah, were among the huge crowd dancing through the marketplace. Saul spotted Aaron and Jason, and a joyous reunion followed, their own personal mob scene of hugs and shouts and happy tears.

"Isn't it great!" Jason exclaimed. "The people are so happy to be able to follow our religion."

"I suppose lots of people are very happy now," said Sarah. She was a calm, cozy woman about the size of Jason's mom, with a shrewd look in her eyes. "But then there are others I'm not so sure about. If keeping our religion had meant so much to them, why did they need to wait for an army to rescue them? Why hadn't they done more themselves to keep it before they let it go?"

"But I don't understand," Jason said. "I've seen some of the terrible things the Syrians have done—"

"You know," Menachem said, "Sarah is right. Even before the Syrian soldiers came and imposed the Greek religion by force, plenty of people were willing to go along with the Greeks who were already here."

Aaron added, with an edge in his voice that Jason hadn't heard before, "That's true, Joseph. Long before the Syrian army, lots of people were willing to give up their religion bit by bit, to take up Greek customs, to say it didn't matter if we altered our ways to be more like theirs or celebrated some of their holidays instead of our own."

Jason suddenly found it difficult to swallow. "Really?" he said.

"Of course," Aaron went on. "They didn't mind giving up their heritage little by little, but then they were surprised when it was all gone. They moan and complain a lot when someone takes it from them, but a lot of them don't do anything to keep it when they have it."

"But maybe now they've learned their lesson," Jason suggested.

"I don't know," said Aaron, "I don't know if people really learn."

"Well, this victory will help them remember," Jason said.

"You think so?" Aaron looked skeptical. "I'm not so sure."

* IX *

NOW THE MACCABEAN ARMY was sweeping toward its final goal, recapturing the holy city of Jerusalem and rededicating the Temple, which the Syrians had grossly defiled. To Jason, the army's advance seemed more like a parade than a movement into battle. All along the route, from the villages and farms they passed, joyous people came to cheer them on. And all along the route, smashed Greek idols showed that freedom had already arrived.

And then, in the distance, Jason saw Jerusalem, golden in the sun. He had been so looking forward to the thrilling sight of the holy city's towers and domes. He remembered the pictures he had seen in books and posters and postcards, but he knew it would look much more grand in reality.

At last he could make out the great and holy

Temple gleaming atop its hill. To Jason, the Temple had existed only as a drawing in a history book because the Jewish buildings on the Temple Mount had been destroyed almost two thousand years before Jason was born. But here, in Judah Maccabee's time, in his friend Aaron's time, in the time of their victorious army, the Temple still stood in its glory.

As the procession approached the city, the mood became more serious. Despite the victory at Bet Tzur, some Syrian forces remained in Jerusalem.

Judah sent ahead an elite squad with orders to surround the small Syrian garrison still holding out within the city walls. They succeeded, and threw the city gates open to the Maccabean army so that they could enter as heroes.

The troops cheered as they approached the entrance to the Holy City, and Jason felt he had never seen or known such pride and happiness. But with his first look at the ancient capital of the Jewish people, his mood abruptly turned, first to surprise, then to disappointment, and finally to horror. The golden, legendary city he had expected to see lay in desolate ruins. The Syrian army had sacked the place, killing the residents or driving them into the hills.

The cheers died on the soldiers' lips as Judah led them through the streets of deserted, burned-out houses and up the hilltop where the Temple stood. The ruins of the City of David spread out below them, the pinkish stones glowing copper in the light of the setting sun.

Jason turned his gaze to the Temple itself. He felt a shiver skitter across his scalp as he remembered how many times, in how many prayers, he had heard it longingly mentioned. All the time he had been approaching the city, the Temple had gleamed like a beacon. It looked dazzling in the brilliant light of Judea, which was somehow much brighter and clearer than the light at home.

The *Kohenim*, the members of the priestly tribe, were entitled to enter the Temple first. Jason knew he could join them, but he hung back. His picture of the ideal Temple struggled against the building he saw before him, which plainly showed years of abuse. At last, though, his curiosity won out and he went inside.

In a great courtyard stood a huge, ugly idol carved from stone. Judah Maccabee stood gazing at it, his proud, determined face deeply lined with sorrow. The fire in the dark eyes had gone out. Jason felt uneasy, as if he had intruded on something very private. But he felt he had to speak.

"General," he said quietly, "doesn't your great victory make you happy?"

Judah's gaze rested on him. "Oh, Joseph, how can I feel joy when I see the Lord's holy Temple in this state? Tell me, did you ever see it in better times?"

"No, sir, never."

"Joseph, in those days it was suitable for the worship of God. It was beautiful, filled with golden implements, rich marble, and the finest weavings. It was clean and lovely. But this—they have built altars to their false gods. They have slaughtered unclean animals on the true altar."

Jason looked about sadly. The general was right. The place was a mess. Garbage and broken crockery lay scattered about. The tapestries hung in filthy tatters. Even the three years the Syrians had held it didn't seem enough time to do so much damage.

"But, General," Jason said at last, "can't we clean it up? Can't we make it right again?"

Judah's eyes seemed to clear. "Ah, my boy, of course we can." To Jason's surprise, the general chuckled softly. "Tell me, Joseph, do you always take such a direct approach to problems? It seems you always do just what has to be done. You bring us supplies when we need them. You become our best spy overnight. You waste no time looking back. You say, 'Can't we make it right?' We could use a thousand like you."

Jason felt proud but very shy. "Gosh, General, I just try to do what I can."

✳ X ✳

JUDAH NEED NOT HAVE WORRIED about the Temple. As word of the newest victory spread, people from miles around converged to help with the cleanup. They scrubbed and washed, painted and brushed. At last the pillars shone, the courtyards gleamed, even the hinges and door handles glistened.

Now everything was ready. The Temple was as clean as human work could make it. Now it was time for the priests to rekindle the eternal light in the great, six-branched menorah and rededicate the Temple to the worship of God.

Jason could hardly wait for the start of the dedication service, called the *Hanukkah* in Hebrew. He had heard it would be magnificent, with singing, and the priests in gorgeous robes, and all the people gathered together.

But then he asked Aaron when it would begin.

And his friend suddenly turned sad, sadder than Jason had ever seen him.

"Dedication?" Aaron said. "There won't be any dedication. It's all off."

"All off? You're crazy!" Jason felt angry, cheated.

"There's not enough oil to light the eternal lamp."

"But there's plenty of oil, Aaron! There's oil all over the place!" Jason remembered seeing many jars and flasks while he was helping with the cleanup.

"No," Aaron said, "they can't use just any oil in the eternal light. To burn there, the oil must be pure, clean, undefiled. It has to be sealed with the mark of the high priest."

"Well, there must be some more. I know there's more!"

"You're the one who's crazy, Joseph."

"Well, I'm not giving up, Aaron. I say we should look for it." He grabbed Aaron's arm. "Listen, I'm going to the Temple to look. Are you coming?"

Aaron said with a grudging laugh, "I guess I'd better. To keep you out of trouble."

"Fat chance," Jason shot back.

So they were off, Aaron skeptical, Jason eager.

When they reached the Temple, they found that

others were already searching its storerooms. The boys joined in.

All the while, though, the priests were becoming more and more convinced that the ceremony would have to be postponed until more oil could be prepared, and that could take weeks.

But Jason was determined. He wanted the dedication now. He knew that if it weren't held soon, he wouldn't get to see it. With the war won and his work over, he had to think about getting back home. He couldn't stick around here forever.

"I wonder if my mom and dad are worried about me," he finally said to Aaron.

"Wow, I'll bet they are," Aaron answered. "You've been with us for quite a while." He turned to look at Jason. "I'd hate to see you go. I'll miss you."

"I'll miss you, too," Jason said. "You—and everybody."

"So you want me to show you how to get to your family?" Aaron asked sadly.

Jason hesitated, torn. He wanted to see his parents, but he was disappointed that he wouldn't get to join in the ceremony that would culminate the Maccabees' struggle.

"I'll stay just a bit longer," he finally said, and threw himself into searching harder than ever. He peered into corners, climbed on chairs to peek over the tops of cabinets, squatted to see under benches. But at last even he decided that there was no hope of finding any oil. If he wanted to see the dedication, he'd have to wait out the days until the new oil was ready.

Wait out the days! Of course he couldn't do that! He was sure Mom and Dad must be frantic. He had left home without any warning. They had no idea where he was. And seeing Menachem and his family, and all the other families, celebrating the victory together, he realized how much he missed his own.

He spotted his backpack lying in the corner where he had dropped it when he started searching. He might as well get his things together, say good-bye to all the friends he had here, and have Aaron take him home. Sadly, he swung the pack onto his back.

And then he saw the bottle. It had been lying near his backpack all the time, but in his excitement he hadn't noticed it before—a small clay jar with a shiny globule of wax at the neck. He picked it up carefully. He wondered if the oil in this newly found jar would be good for burning. Would it be any more suitable for burning in the Temple's sacred menorah than all the other oil jars that had already been found, exam⁄ined, and rejected as impure?

"Aaron!" he said, "look at this. Is this bottle good?"

Aaron took the jar and looked closely at the wax that served as its stopper. Then he yelled a joyous "Yes!" There was the seal of the high priest, whole and unbroken. There, bitten deep into the wax, was the mark that meant the dedication could go on!

Jason took the jar back and dashed out into the courtyard. There, Judah, his arms held high, was shouting to a throng of waiting people, "...can't go on until the oil is ready. There is nothing else we can do."

A moan of disappointment filled the courtyard as Jason and Aaron raced toward the general.

"No, sir! Wait! I found it!" Jason thrust the precious flask into the hands of the startled Judah Maccabee. "Look, General, it's good! The seal is unbroken!"

The moan became a huge cheer.

Judah tried to wave the crowd silent, but cheer after cheer rose from the people.

"This is only a small flask," Judah shouted over

the din. "It will only last a short time."

"Go ahead anyway!" yelled a voice from the crowd, echoing what was in Jason's heart. Other voices took up the cry until it surged like a wave against the walls of the courtyard.

The high priest stepped forward in his long white robe and jeweled breastplate. Jason held the flask to him, his eyes questioning. The priest smiled back, then nodded. As the shouting rose to a joyous, deafening crescendo, he turned and led the way into the Temple.

Then the high priest lit the great stone menorah with the pure oil and led the people in prayers of thanksgiving, even though many in the crowd said that the fuel from the little flask couldn't last very long.

But the oil burned and burned and just kept burning, and word of it spread. And soon the whole city, the whole world, it seemed, was singing and dancing and feasting. The celebrating went on, and before Jason knew it, the flames had lasted for a whole day, and Jason knew they would last and last.

"It's like a miracle," Aaron said. "That oil is still burning."

"But the whole thing is a miracle," Jason replied.

"Winning the war, freeing the Temple, finding the oil. It's *all* a miracle."

Judah, who had overheard them, came toward them and said, "That's true, Joseph." And when he smiled, Jason saw again the same bold, inspiring expression the great leader had worn the first time they had met. "We must be very grateful that we were able to win this victory, and that our people will be able to enjoy freedom, and that we were able to restore the Temple to the service of God. We must always remember to be thankful for what has happened."

"Oh, we will, General," Jason said. "People will remember this day forever."

Judah laughed. "It's kind of you to say so, Joseph, but I think you're exaggerating a bit. People don't have such long memories."

"No, General, I'm sure of it. Thousands of years from now, people will still be celebrating your victory. They'll be singing songs and telling stories about it."

"Thousands of years from now?" Judah said. "Now, *that* would be a miracle."

✷ XI ✷

JASON OPENED HIS EYES and blinked. It was morning, and he was lying in his own bed, in his own room, at home. He could hear the water running in the sink down the hall. Dad must be getting ready for work.

He sat up and scratched his head. Where was Aaron? Where was Judah? How did he get back?

"Are you awake, son?" Dad was standing in the doorway in his bathrobe. "It sounded like you might be. Can I come in for a minute?"

"Sure, Dad."

"Jason, I wanted to talk with you. You seemed upset last night."

"Last night?"

"Yes—the first night of Hanukkah."

"The first night?"

His father gave Jason a strange look. "Are you feel-ing all right?"

"Sure, Dad." Jason swallowed hard. "Uh—what's up?"

"Well, I know that this Christmas business upsets you. And I know that you think I'm being un-reasonable about it. But I want you to try to under-stand how I feel. I just think that doing what you want me to do would be wrong."

"I know, Dad. You don't want us to give up our heritage bit by bit. If we do, before we know it, it will be gone. And we will forget."

His father stared at him. "Why, that's exactly what I think. I couldn't say it better. It's important to remember the miracle."

"The miracle, Dad?"

"You know, the oil, the lights, the victory—"

"I guess that was a miracle, Dad."

"You don't think so?"

"Of course I do." He thought of Judah and Aaron, of marching in the mountains and dancing in the streets. He thought of Judah's last words to him. And of himself, here at home. "But it's not the most important one. Dad, do you know what the real miracle of Hanukkah is?"

His father shook his head.

"The real miracle of Hanukkah," Jason said, "is that after so many years, we still remember."

✳

A Note on the History

The tradition of Hanukkah, which means "dedication" in Hebrew, arose out of the struggle between
the emperor Antiochus IV and a Jewish rebel force led
by the priest Mattathias and his family. Although
Antiochus was a Syrian ruler, he enforced the Greek
religions and customs that were the legacy of the Greek
emperor Alexander the Great. Hundreds of years
before, Alexander had conquered a huge empire that
stretched from Greece into India and North Africa
and included the ancient land of Judea, home of
Jerusalem and the Jewish people.

After Alexander died in 323 B.C.E., the empire was
divided. The area that contained Judea and neighbor-
ing Palestine was ruled by a line of Syrian emperors
known as the Seleucid dynasty. Under Seleucid rule,
Greek culture and the pagan Greek religion gained
increasing influence throughout their empire. Greek
ways were at odds with a number of the beliefs and
practices of Judaism, but many people, including some
Jews, adopted various Greek customs. For several years
the Jewish religion was permitted, however, and

Jewish worship continued at the Temple in Jerusalem.

When Antiochus IV came to power in 175 B.C.E., though, he felt that the empire would not be unified as long as some of his subjects continued to practice Judaism. Under his orders, a statue of Zeus was built in the Temple and, starting in 167 B.C.E., Greek sacrifices were performed there. At the same time, the government authorities tried to force the Jewish people to give up Judaism and adopt the Greek religion. Some Jews obeyed, but others refused. Jews who resisted were tortured and killed.

Mattathias, a devout Jew, fled to the hills with his sons and a band of followers, and together they took up arms against the Syrian army. Eventually his son Judah the Maccabee commanded the rebels, and they came to be known by their leader's name—*Maccabee*, which meant "the Hammer." Their fight against the Syrians lasted three years, and the battle against Gorgias's troops was one of four major battles in the war. In 164 B.C.E., the Maccabees finally conquered Jerusalem and won back the Temple. During the Jewish month of Kislev, which corresponds to December, they cleansed and rededicated the Temple to Jewish worship.

The Books of Maccabees, which tell the entire story of this war, are not part of the Hebrew Bible. Instead they belong to a group of nonsacred writings known as the Apocrypha.

During the years of Syrian conflict, copies of the Book of Daniel circulated among the Jewish people. Since the book told the story of Jews withstanding persecution in the much earlier Babylonian exile, some thought the book was hundreds of years old. However, modern scholars believe that it was a new book at the time of Antiochus IV's reign, written in order to inspire the Jews struggling to keep their religion alive in the face of Syrian opposition.

✷

A Note on the Math

While a modern twelve-year-old like Jason is able to multiply with ease, the ancient numerical systems of Aaron's time were not very practical for doing calculations.

In the Hebrew system, numbers were represented by letters of the Hebrew alphabet: *aleph* stood for 1, *bet* stood for 2, *gimel* for 3, and so on, up to 10. A different set of letters was used to denote values such as 20, 30, and 40; still other letters were needed for 100, 200, 300, and the like. Then, when necessary, the letters were combined. Here's the symbol for 100, the Hebrew letter *koph*:

This seems simple enough. However, it would take even more symbols to express a number like 126:

| vav | khaph | koph |

In this figure, *koph* is combined with *khaph*, which represents 20, and *vav*, 6. (Hebrew is read from right to left.) This method of stringing letters together is similar to the Roman numeral system, where C represents 100, X is 10, V is 5, I is 1—and 126 is CXXVI!

What made both the Hebrew and the Roman systems troublesome was that there was no consistency to how many letters were used to form a number. For instance, while 130 is clearly a larger number than 126, in Hebrew numerals it contains *fewer* symbols: *lamed* (for 30) and *koph*.

This inconsistency made it impossible to do math problems the way we do them today. That is, we write one number beneath another so that their positions line up properly, and then we compute them. We can do this because our number system relies on a concept called *place value.* We know that whole numbers 10 through 99 will always have only two digits—a digit in the "ones" position and another in the "tens" position—and numbers from 100 to 999 will always include a third digit in the "hundreds" position. In the Hebrew and Roman systems, though, there was no way to line up numbers by ones or tens or hundreds, and as a result, mathematical functions were incredibly difficult—even more so during a time when writing materials were scarce!

The real "miracle," of course, was made by the Indian and Arab mathematicians who developed the number system we use today.

∗

BERYL LIEFF BENDERLY makes her children's book debut with *Jason's Miracle: A Hanukkah Story*. She is a prize-winning health and psychology writer who has written or co-authored six books for adults, and she regularly contributes to national magazines, newspapers, and web sites. She lives with her family in Washington, D.C.